MY FIRST LITTLE HOUSE BOOKS

WINTER DAYS

❧ IN THE ❧

BIG WOODS

ADAPTED FROM THE LITTLE HOUSE BOOKS

By Laura Ingalls Wilder

Illustrated by Renée Graef

BARNES
&NOBLE
BOOKS
NEW YORK

For Tim
—R.G.

Winter Days in the Big Woods Text adapted from Little House in the Big Woods, copyright 1932 by Laura Ingalls Wilder,
renewed 1959 by Roger Lea MacBride Illustrations copyright © 1994 by Renée Graef Printed in the U.S.A. All rights reserved.
Library of Congress Cataloging-in-Publication Data Wilder, Laura Ingalls, 1867-1957. Winter Days in the Big Woods / adapted from
the little house books by Laura Ingalls Wilder ; illustrated by Renée Graef. p. cm. — (My first little house books)
Summary: A young pioneer girl and her family spend the winter in their log cabin in the Big Woods of Wisconsin.
ISBN 0-06-023014-2. — ISBN 0-06-023022-3 (lib. bdg.) —ISBN 0-694-00876-1 (pbk.)
[1. Frontier and pioneer life—Wisconsin—Fiction. 2. Family life—Wisconsin—Fiction. 3. Wisconsin—Fiction.]
I. Graef, Renée, ill. II. Title. III. Series. PZ7.W6461WI 1994 [E]—dc20 93-45883 CIP AC
HarperCollins®, 📖®, HarperFestival®, and Little House® are trademarks of HarperCollins Publishers Inc.

Illustrations for the My First Little House Books are inspired by the work of Garth Williams with his permission, which we gratefully acknowledge.

Once upon a time, a little girl named Laura
lived in the Big Woods of Wisconsin in a little
house made of logs.

Laura lived in the little house with her Pa, her Ma, her big sister Mary, her baby sister Carrie, and their good old bulldog Jack.

Winter was coming to the Big Woods. Soon the little house would be covered with snow. Pa went hunting every day so that they would have meat during the long, cold winter.

Ma, Laura, and Mary gathered potatoes and carrots, beets and turnips, cabbages and onions, and peppers and pumpkins from the garden next to the little house.

By the time winter came, the little house was full of good things to eat. Laura and Mary thought the attic was a lovely place to play. They played house by using the round orange pumpkins as tables and chairs, and everything was snug and cozy.

Soon the first snow came, and it was very cold. In the mornings the windows were covered with beautiful frost pictures of trees and flowers and fairies. Ma said that Jack Frost came in the night and made the pictures while everyone was asleep. Laura and Mary were allowed to use Ma's thimble to make pretty patterns of circles in the frost.

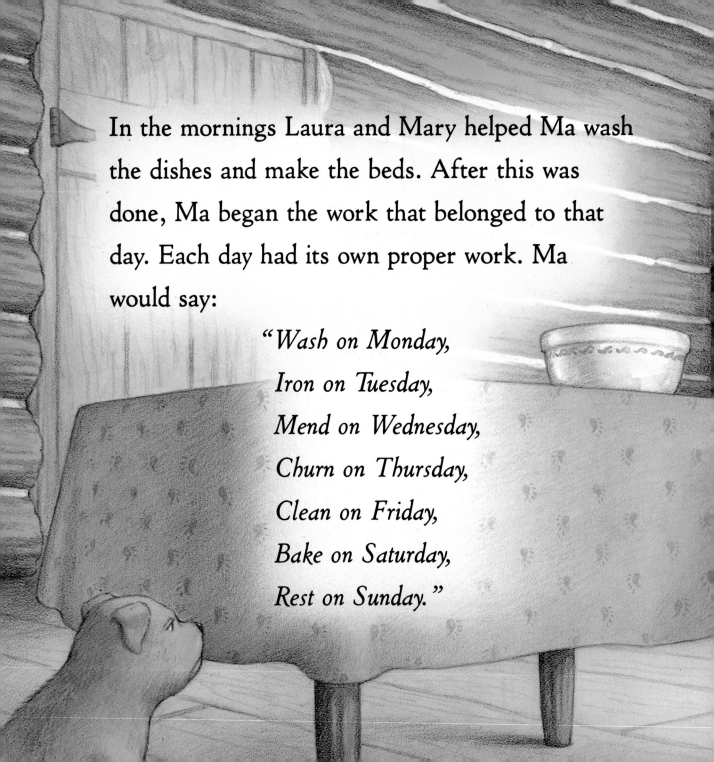

In the mornings Laura and Mary helped Ma wash the dishes and make the beds. After this was done, Ma began the work that belonged to that day. Each day had its own proper work. Ma would say:

> *"Wash on Monday,*
> *Iron on Tuesday,*
> *Mend on Wednesday,*
> *Churn on Thursday,*
> *Clean on Friday,*
> *Bake on Saturday,*
> *Rest on Sunday."*

Laura liked the churning and baking days best of all. Ma had to churn the cream for a long time until it turned into butter. Mary could sometimes churn while Ma rested, but Laura was too little.

On Saturdays, when Ma made the bread, Laura
and Mary each had a little piece of dough to make

into a little loaf. Ma even gave them a bit of
cookie dough to make little cookies.

After the day's work was done, Ma would sometimes cut out paper dolls for Laura and Mary. She
drew their faces on with a pencil, and cut dresses,
hats, and ribbons out of colored paper so that
Mary and Laura could dress their dolls beautifully.

But the best time of all was at night, when Pa came home. He would throw off his fur cap and coat and mittens and call, "Where's my little half-pint of sweet cider half drunk up?" That was Laura, because she was so small.

Sometimes Pa would take down his fiddle and
sing. Pa would keep time with his foot. Laura and
Mary would clap their hands to the music when he
sang:

"Yankee Doodle went to town,
He wore his striped trousies,
He swore he couldn't see the town,
There was so many houses."

Other times Pa would tell stories. When Laura
and Mary begged him for a story, he would take
them on his knees and tickle their faces with his
long whiskers until they laughed out loud. His
eyes were blue and merry.

Outside it was cold and snowy, but the little log cabin was snug and cozy. Pa, Ma, Laura, Mary,

and Baby Carrie were comfortable and happy in their little house in the Big Woods.

MY FIRST LITTLE HOUSE BOOKS

CHRISTMAS
IN THE
BIG WOODS

ADAPTED FROM THE LITTLE HOUSE BOOKS

By Laura Ingalls Wilder

Illustrated by Renée Graef

BARNES
&NOBLE
BOOKS
NEW YORK

Reprinted with permission of HarperCollins Publishers

For my Dad
—R.G.

Christmas in the Big Woods   Text adapted from Little House in the Big Woods, *copyright 1932 by Laura Ingalls Wilder,*
renewed 1959 by Roger Lea MacBride.   Illustrations copyright © 1995 by Renée Graef.   Printed in the U.S.A. All rights reserved.
Library of Congress Cataloging-in-Publication Data   Wilder, Laura Ingalls, 1867–1957.   Christmas in the Big Woods / adapted from
the little house books by Laura Ingalls Wilder ; illustrated by Renée Graef.   p.   cm.   — (My first little house books)
Summary: A young pioneer girl and her family celebrate Christmas in their cabin in the Wisconsin woods.   ISBN 0-06-024752-5.
— ISBN 0-06-024753-3 (lib. bdg.) — ISBN 0-694-00877-X (pbk.) [1. Christmas—Fiction.   2. Frontier and pioneer life—
Wisconsin—Fiction.   3. Family life—Wisconsin—Fiction.   4. Wisconsin—Fiction] I. Graef, Renée, ill.   II. Series.
PZ7.W6461Ch 1995 E—dc20 94-14478   CIP   AC
HarperCollins®, ■®, *HarperFestival®, and Little House are trademarks of HarperCollins Publishers Inc.*

Illustrations for the My First Little House Books are inspired by the work of Garth Williams with his permission, which we gratefully acknowledge.

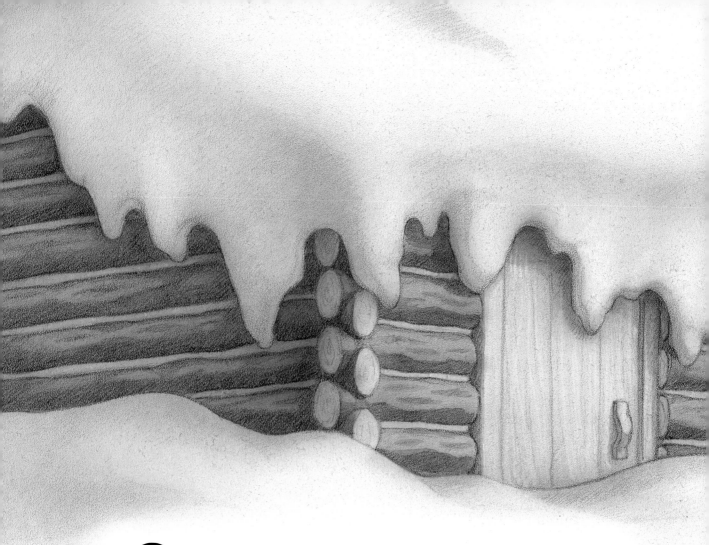

Once upon a time, a little girl named Laura
lived in the Big Woods of Wisconsin in a little
house made of logs.

Laura lived in the little house with her Pa, her Ma, her big sister Mary, her little sister Carrie, and their good old bulldog Jack.

Christmas was coming, and the little house was covered with snow. When Pa came in from shoveling, he caught Laura up in a big bear hug against his cold winter coat. His mustache was covered with melting snowflakes.

Ma was busy all day long cooking good things for Christmas. She baked bread and apple pies, and filled a big jar with cookies. Laura and Mary got to lick the spoon.

Pa and Ma showed Laura and Mary how to make
molasses candy by pouring hot sugar-and-molasses
syrup into pans of snow. The syrup hardened at
once and turned into candy! Laura and Mary
could eat one piece each, but the rest was saved
for Christmas Day.

The day before Christmas, Aunt Eliza, Uncle Peter, and cousins Peter, Alice, and Ella came to visit. Laura and Mary heard sleigh bells ringing, and then a big bobsled came out of the woods. Aunt Eliza, Uncle Peter, and the cousins were inside covered up with blankets.

When everyone came inside, the little house was filled to the seams. Jack ran around in circles, barking happily. Now there were lots of children to play with!

Laura and Mary and the cousins put on their
warm coats and mittens and scarves and went
outside to make pictures in the soft, deep snow.

They played so hard that when night came, they were too excited to sleep. But they knew they must, or Santa Claus would not come. So they hung their stockings by the fireplace, put on their red flannel nightgowns, and went to bed.

In the morning they all woke up almost at the same moment and ran to see what was in their stockings. In every stocking was a pair of bright red mittens and a stick of red-and-white-striped peppermint candy. They were so happy they could hardly speak.

But Laura was the happiest of all. In her stocking
was a beautiful rag doll with black button eyes
and a pink-and-blue calico dress. Laura named her
doll Charlotte, and she let all the other children
hold her.

For Christmas breakfast Ma made each child a
pancake man. All the children held their plates
next to the stove and watched while Ma made the
pancake men one by one out of pancake batter.
Peter ate his up right away, but the girls ate theirs
slowly to make them last.

It was too cold to go outside, so the children played quietly inside. They ate their candy, admired their mittens, and looked at the pictures in Pa's big green book until it was time for the cousins to go home. Laura held Charlotte in her arms the whole time.

At last Aunt Eliza, Uncle Peter, and the cousins bundled up in their coats and blankets and got into the bobsled. "Good-by!" they called, and off they went into the woods. In a little while the happy sound of sleigh bells was gone, and Christmas was over. But what a happy Christmas it had been!

LITTLE HOUSE

Laura Ingalls Wilder

MY FIRST LITTLE HOUSE BOOKS

DANCE AT GRANDPA'S

ADAPTED FROM THE LITTLE HOUSE BOOKS

By Laura Ingalls Wilder

Illustrated by Renée Graef

BARNES & NOBLE BOOKS
NEW YORK

For Rhonda
—R.G.

Dance at Grandpa's   Text adapted from Little House in the Big Woods, copyright 1932 by Laura Ingalls Wilder,
renewed 1959 by Roger Lea MacBride   Illustrations copyright © 1994 by Renée Graef   Printed in the U.S.A. All rights reserved.
Library of Congress Cataloging-in-Publication Data   Wilder, Laura Ingalls, 1867–1957.   Dance at Grandpa's / adapted from
the little house books by Laura Ingalls Wilder ; illustrated by Renée Graef.   p.   cm. — (My first little house books)
Summary: A young pioneer girl and her family attend a wintertime party at her grandparents' house in the Big Woods of Wisconsin.
ISBN 0-06-023878-X.— ISBN 0-06-023879-8 (lib. bdg.) —ISBN 0-694-00885-0 (pbk.)
[1. Frontier and pioneer life—Wisconsin—Fiction.   2. Family life—Wisconsin—Fiction.   3. Parties—Fiction.   4. Wisconsin—Fiction.]
I. Graef, Renée, ill.   II. Title.   III. Series: Wilder, Laura Ingalls, 1867–1957. My first Little House books.
PZ7.W6461Dan 1994   [E]—dc20   93-24535   CIP   AC
HarperCollins®, ▰®, HarperFestival®, and Little House® are trademarks of HarperCollins Publishers Inc.

Illustrations for the My First Little House Books are inspired by the work of Garth Williams with his permission, which we gratefully acknowledge.

Once upon a time, a little girl named Laura lived in the Big Woods of Wisconsin in a little house made of logs. She lived there with her Pa, her Ma, her big sister Mary, her baby sister Carrie, and their good old bulldog Jack.

One winter morning everyone got up early, for there was going to be a big party at Grandpa's house. While Laura and Mary ate their breakfast, Pa packed his fiddle carefully in its box and put it in the big sled waiting by the gate.

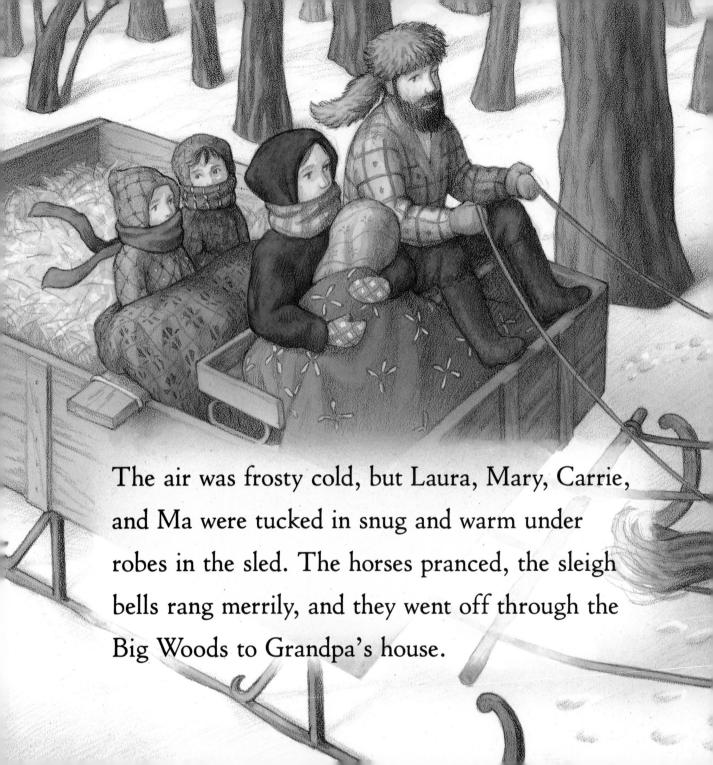

The air was frosty cold, but Laura, Mary, Carrie, and Ma were tucked in snug and warm under robes in the sled. The horses pranced, the sleigh bells rang merrily, and they went off through the Big Woods to Grandpa's house.

It did not seem long before they were sweeping
into the clearing at Grandpa's house. Grandma
stood at the door smiling and calling them to
come in.

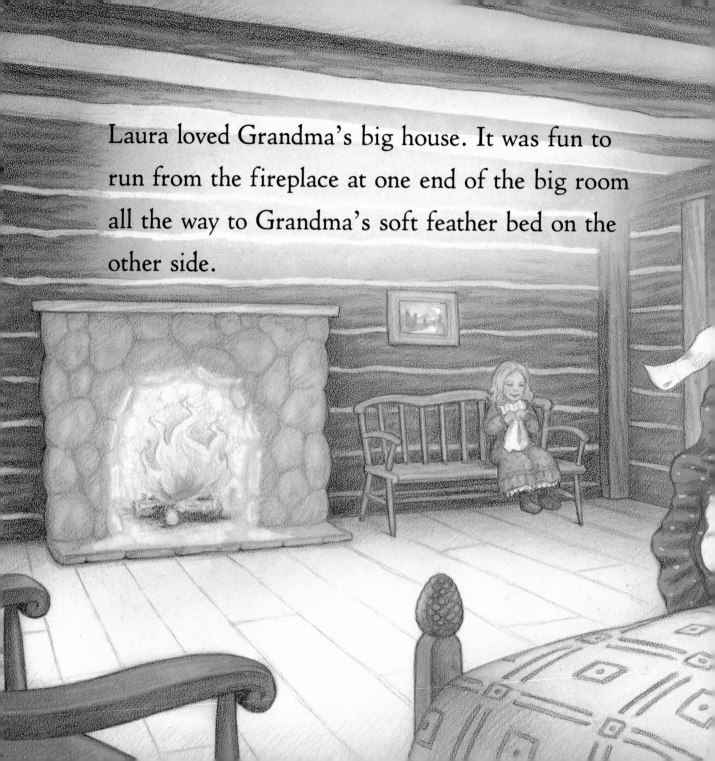

Laura loved Grandma's big house. It was fun to run from the fireplace at one end of the big room all the way to Grandma's soft feather bed on the other side.

The whole house smelled good. There were sweet and spicy smells coming from the kitchen, and the smell of hickory logs burning with bright, clear flames in the fireplace.

Before long it was time to get ready for the party. Laura watched while Ma and the aunts made themselves pretty. They combed their long hair and put on their best dresses. Laura thought Ma was the most beautiful of all in her green ruffled dress.

Soon people began to come to the party. They
came on foot through the woods with their
lanterns, and they came in sleds and wagons.
Sleigh bells were jingling all the time.

The big room was filled with tall boots and
swishing skirts, and there were ever so many babies
lying in rows on Grandma's feather bed. Laura
thought Baby Carrie was the prettiest.

Then Pa took out his fiddle and began to play. All the skirts began to swirl and all the boots began to stamp. "Swing your partners!" Pa called.

Laura watched Ma's skirt swaying and her dark head bowing and thought she was the loveliest dancer in the world.

Soon it was time for dinner. The long table was loaded with pumpkin pies, dried-berry pies, and cookies. There was cold boiled pork and salt-rising bread. How sour the pickles were! They all ate until they could eat no more.

The fiddling and dancing went on and on until
it was time for Laura and the other children to go
to bed.

When Laura woke up, it was morning. There were pancakes and maple syrup for breakfast, and then Pa brought the horses and sled to the door.

Pa tucked Laura and Mary and Carrie and Ma into the sled. Grandma and Grandpa stood calling, "Good-by! Good-by!" as they rode away into the Big Woods, going home. What a wonderful party it had been!